Jack and the Jungle

MALACHY DOYLE

ILLUSTRATED BY PADDY DONNELLY

D1584023

BLOOMSBURY EDUCATION
Bloomsbury Publishing Plc
50 Bedford Square, London, WC1B 3DP, UK

BLOOMSBURY, BLOOMSBURY EDUCATION and the Diana logo are
trademarks of Bloomsbury Publishing Plc

First published in Great Britain in 2010 by A & C Black, an imprint of Bloomsbury Publishing Plc

This edition published in Great Britain in 2019 by Bloomsbury Publishing plc

Text copyright © Malachy Doyle, 2010
Illustrations copyright © Paddy Donnelly, 2019

Malachy Doyle and Paddy Donnelly have asserted their rights under the Copyright,
Designs and Patents Act, 1988, to be identified as Author and Illustrator of this work

This is a work of fiction. Names and characters are the product of the author's imagination and
any resemblance to actual persons, living or dead, is entirely coincidental.

All rights reserved. No part of this publication may be reproduced or transmitted in any form or
by any means, electronic or mechanical, including photocopying, recording, or any information
storage or retrieval system, without prior permission in writing from the publishers.

A catalogue record for this book is available from the British Library

ISBN: PB: 978-1-4729-5961-4; ePDF: 978-1-4729-5960-7; ePub: 978-1-4729-5959-1;
enhanced ePub: 978-1-4729-6947-7

2 4 6 8 10 9 7 5 3 1

Printed and bound in China by Leo Paper Products

All papers used by Bloomsbury Publishing Plc are natural, recyclable products from wood grown
in well managed forests. The manufacturing processes conform to the environmental regulations of
the country of origin.

To find out more about our authors and books visit www.bloomsbury.com
and sign up for our newsletters

Chapter One

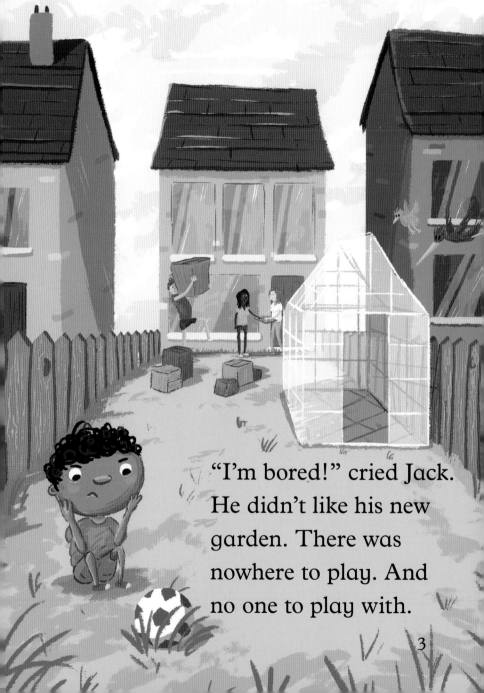

"I'm bored!" cried Jack. He didn't like his new garden. There was nowhere to play. And no one to play with.

"I'M BORED!" he roared.
Then he saw a ball, lying on the grass.
He swung back his foot and knocked it
against the wall.
But he kicked the ball too hard.

It went high, into the air…
It flew over the top of the
wall, and landed in the
next garden.

Only it wasn't a garden. He'd seen it from the house. It was full of trees and creepers, and it was more like a jungle!

"Oh no," said Jack. "It's probably full of wild animals. How am I going to get my ball back?"

He found a box and put it
beside the wall. But it was
too high to climb…

It was too high even to see over.
"Hello," said Jack. "Is anyone there?"
But there was no answer.
"Hello," he said, a bit louder. "Can
I have my ball back, please?"
There was still no answer.

Chapter Two

Suddenly, Jack heard a voice.
"Over here!" it said.
He looked around,
but he couldn't
see anyone.

"Up here!" cried the voice.
Jack looked up, into the
trees. And saw a face,
smiling down at him.

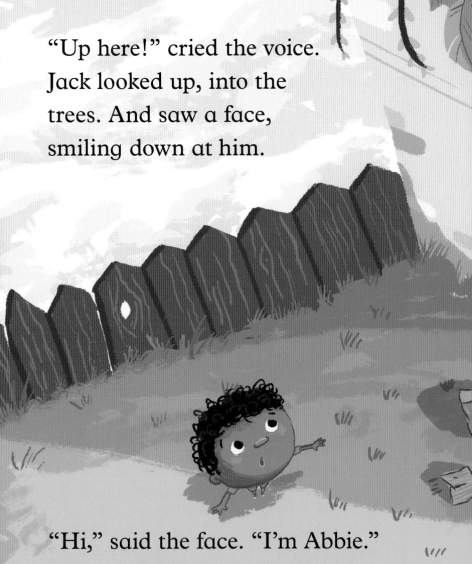

"Hi," said the face. "I'm Abbie."
It was a face full of freckles. Freckles
and red hair.
"I'm Jack," said Jack. "Have you seen my
ball? I kicked it over the wall, by mistake."

"No," said Abbie. "I was too busy chasing snakes. But I'll go and have a look for it, if you want."

11

Jack was worried. He didn't like snakes.
They were all slimy, and sometimes
they bit people.

Then Abbie waved to him from another
tree, further down the wall.
"I can see your ball, Jack," she called.
"But I have some bad news for you…"

"What?" asked Jack.
"A wolf has got it!" said Abbie.
"A deadly, dangerous wolf."

Chapter Three

Jack didn't know what to say.
"Stay there a minute," said Abbie.
"I'll go and get it off him."
"Be careful," said Jack, under his
breath. "Wolves bite."

Jack could hear Abbie fighting the wolf.
It was quite a struggle.

At last there was a thud, and the ball came through the trees.
It flew over the wall and bounced next to Jack. It nearly hit his dad's new greenhouse.

"I've sorted out the wolf!" cried Abbie, from deep within the jungle. "But there's more bad news…"

"Oh dear," said Jack. "What is it now?" "Three tigers are coming towards me," she shouted. "Three tigers with very sharp teeth!"

"Oh no!" Jack covered his ears. He didn't want to hear her being eaten by a tiger. "Abbie, Abbie, where are you?" he said, after a while. "Are you all right?"

"I'm fine," came the answer. "I escaped
from the tigers, but..."
"But what?"
"But now there's a giant coming,"
said Abbie. "A great hungry giant!"

Chapter Four

"Help!" moaned Jack.

He crouched down behind the wall.

He stayed there for a long time.

Everything was silent. And he couldn't

see a thing with his eyes tight shut.

Suddenly, he heard a creaking sound.
A hand touched him on the shoulder
and he nearly jumped out of his skin.
"It's all right, Jack," said a soft voice.
"Follow me."
It was Abbie!

She showed him a door in the wall.
It was so hidden by spiky things that
Jack hadn't seen it before.

Jack didn't really want to go into the jungle. But Abbie took him by the hand and led him through the door.
She was whistling!

Trees and tall grasses pressed in, all around them.

Jack kept his eyes on the ground to make sure he didn't stand on a snake.

But he had to look up, every now and again, in case there were any wolves or tigers or giants.

Chapter Five

At last, they came to the edge of
the jungle.

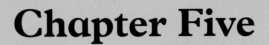

In front of them was
a pond. A woman was sitting
on the other side. She was laying
out a picnic on the grass. Beside
her were a dog and three cats.

The dog came bounding over, wagging
its tail.
"Guess who this is, Jack…" said
Abbie, laughing.

Jack didn't know what to say.

"It's the WOLF!" cried Abbie. "And guess who these are," she said, pointing at the cats.

"The three tigers?" said Jack.
Abbie nodded. "This is the GIANT..." she said, pointing to the woman.

"And this is the SNAKE!" she cried, picking up a hosepipe and spraying water all over him.

"Hello, Jack. I'm Abbie's mum," said
the giant, smiling. "I hope my daughter
hasn't been teasing you."
"Sorry, Jack," said Abbie, grinning.
"I was only teasing because I like you."

Jack sat down in the sunshine to dry off. The giant gave him some lemonade and a big slice of carrot cake. The wolf licked his face. The tigers curled up on his lap, and Jack was happy.

It was only the first day in his new house and already he'd found a friend. A friend and a jungle full of animals!